Pen of
Iniquity

Deno Sandz

PublishAmerica
Baltimore

© 2009 by Deno Sandz.
All rights reserved. No part of this book may be reproduced, stored in a retrieval system or transmitted in any form or by any means without the prior written permission of the publishers, except by a reviewer who may quote brief passages in a review to be printed in a newspaper, magazine or journal.

First printing

All characters in this book are fictitious, and any resemblance to real persons, living or dead, is coincidental.

PublishAmerica has allowed this work to remain exactly as the author intended, verbatim, without editorial input.

ISBN: 1-60813-073-8
PUBLISHED BY PUBLISHAMERICA, LLLP
www.publishamerica.com
Baltimore

Printed in the United States of America

Chapter 1

In 1998 on the brink of the rising percentage of men and women sent to prison. Northville Prison located off Florida's Northern coast, in the small town of Northville was closing down. Twenty percent of the working people worked at the prison accounting for fifty percent of the town's economic base.

The citizens battled with the prison for a short time, but the prison would soon close.

Inmate Daniel Gordon contributed to the confusion inside. He informed the outside news media regarding the corruption and conditions behind the walls of Northville. His allegations consisted of drug smuggling, guard brutality, health issues, murder, prostitution, mess hall conditions, and infirmary conditions.

The definition of the word *saint* hid itself from Daniel's heart. His crimes on the outside showed this. He was a killer. But after, arriving at Northville

Prison he changed using his mind, instead of his emotional anger, seeking peace in his life while helping Northville Prison inmates.

Daniel trusted his cellmate Chris with his outside communication with the media. Chris was incarcerated for statutory rape, assault, and attempted murder.

Chris spied for the warden without suspension from Daniel. The Warden informed his guards, and the guards informed the inmates who worked for the warden. They believed that the information leaked to the outside influenced the closing of the prison and the loss of their jobs.

Two days after the Warden received the stunning news. He held a meeting before lights out with everyone involved and they agreed to murder Daniel Gordon.

Around ten o'clock that night the tier guard called lights out and made his first check around twelve.

Fifteen minutes pass twelve the clock showed. Suddenly, the guards moved quietly towards Daniel's cell passing the cell of inmate-158852, Ronald Grimms, his friend since the first day Daniel walked into Northville prison. His insight on life, religion, and faith influenced Daniel, making them trusting friends. Near the darkest corner of the cell bars Ronald kneeled down wanting desperately to alert Daniel. Tears plummeting down his face, as he listened. Knowing his friend would parish.

Twenty years ago Grimms committed a heinous crime. His wife had lied about bruises on her body he had discovered. She accused the preacher of their small church in Alabama of rape. Out of rage, Ronald stormed the church and murdered her lover with his bare hands.

Based on a lie, a jury of Ronald's peers sentenced him to life in prison.

Chapter 2

Through the darkness of the cell block the guards proceeded with the green flood lights on the walls shining off their high glossed boots. Cell-D25: "Daniel Gordon's house."

Guard Wanton shined his flash light four times through the darkness to another guard standing by the cell door release lever at the entrance to the tier. Slowly, Grimms placed a mirror through his bars to see the faces of his friend's attackers making certain that his mirror did not cast a noticeable glare which would condemn him.

The cell gate rolled open. Chris knew the outcome while he faked being asleep. He couldn't risk the forbidden word snitch to stimulate the ears of the other inmates.

Moving in with lightening speed and precision the guards quietly taped Daniel's mouth, hands, and feet. Chris eased back into the corner of his bed. Two guards pulled Daniel out of his bunk while the others grabbed Chris and held him down. An inmate standing outside of the cell walked in sticking into Chris's arm a syringe of pure heroine.

The guards and the inmates left Chris their in his bunk with saliva dripping out of his mouth, dead from an over dose. Daniel struggled with the guards and noticed Chris's eyeballs. Daniel's facial expression never showed emotion.

Finally, the guards made it impossible for Daniel to move. Through his mirror, Grimms was witnessing everything. Suddenly, Ronald fumbled the mirror grabbing it before it hit the floor catching the attention of a guard. Slowly, he walked to Cell: D29 flashing his light inside. Quickly, Ronald fell on his bunk and covered his head. Finally, the guard walked away. Softly, Ronald spoke, "Good-bye my friend, I'm sorry."

Chapter 3

Daniel's path to death started down a dark flight of stairs that led to an even darker stairway, leading to a tunnel. At the end of the tunnel was the boiler room. Awaiting there was the Warden Verdana, more guards, and more inmates. Pipes protruded through the walls on every angle. In the corner stood the boiler and steam from the cracked pipes made a hissing sound. The evil men dropped Daniel in the middle of the room to view his fear. Warden Verdana bent down, ripped the tape from his mouth, and stepped on his hand.

"You have a lot to say, so say it now," Verdana urged. Daniel looked around at all the faces as if taking photographs.

Without warning,, Verdana kicked Daniel in his head and spoke, "You have nothing to say." With a stare of hatred and of redemption Daniel replied.

"All right boys," Verdana roared. The guards and inmates began beating Daniel until he bleed from his ears. Then, hung him on the steam pipe and opened it.

Barely alive, Daniel eyes gazed upon the shadow of death prancing around the boiler room. However, his outraged soul could not be controlled or captured by death. The intense force of steam striped the skin from his bones as they opened the pipe valve. After five minutes they closed the valve laughing and joking around as Daniel faded into the after life.

"What to do now?" a guard asked.

"Throw him in the furnace, along with these records of his imprisonment," Warden Verdana ordered. Down off the pipe they pulled him.

Suddenly, Daniel raised his head and spoke, "I shall remember you all." Surprised, the guards dropped Daniel standing there watching as Daniel's eyes closed. Then, they dragged Daniel to the furnace unaware of the small bible that fell from his pocket smoking like a fired gun. They through Daniel Gordon in and closed the gate. Rejoicing again, they started to walk away. Then, a loud screech emanated from the furnace. Daniel was still alive, as the fire consumed him holding on to the gate. Warden Verdana's body froze, as he gazed into the eyes of death. The guards and inmates curried into the tunnel. Abandoned and alone Warden Verdana stood looking at Daniel as his hands slid down the gate. Slowly, Warden Verdana turned and walked away.

Suddenly, "I shall remember you all," roared through the tunnel from Daniel's tormenting soul, shaking the foundation of the prison as the Warden's footsteps echoed through the darkness.

The prison closed down the next day and Daniel Gordon's book of life had been closed.

Chapter 4

Blue skies and the warm breeze made it a beautiful day for a prison closing. Chained and escorted by prison guards the inmates were lead out of the prison. Mothers, fathers, sons, daughters, and wives caught a glimpse of them. Inmates listened for their name and number to make sure they boarded the right bus.

Patiently, Daniel's mother Gale stood listening for her son's name. Unknowingly, Gale walked over to a guard who had something to do with her son's murder and asked him about Daniel.

Deceitfully, he checked his list finding no Daniel Gordon on it.

"What! You mean he transferred earlier in the week without me knowing," she argued.

"No, Ms. Gordon, he has never been here," the guard explained.

"That's impossible, I just saw him last week during visitation," she yelled.

"Take that up with the Warden maim," the rude guard answered.

"Ronald Grimms," the guard shouted. Gale turned, remembering the name from letters Daniel had written her as their eyes connected.

"Mr. Grimms, Mr. Grimms, have you seen my son Daniel?" Ms. Gordon asked.

"Grimms on the bus," the guard spoke. With pain in his eyes Grimms stared as he boarded the bus leaving Gale there alone and confused.

She started walking towards her car and inside a gust of wind she heard…a voice. Instantly, tears poured down her face and her southern spirit detected an unrest soul. As luck would have it, she stumbled into the Warden walking to his car.

"Warden Verdana, my son Daniel. Do you know him?"

"Daniel maim, I do not believe I know of such an inmate."

"Did you ask the guards?" the Warden spoke.

"Yes I did," Gale answered.

"Well, maim if they said there's no record, there's no record, good day," the Warden spoke rudely. Ms. Gordon watched as the Warden departed the abandoned prison still having no idea of the whereabouts of her son.

Gale hired an investigator, went to prison officials, made numerous phone calls, and even hired a lawyer. However, Daniel never was found leaving her penniless. Ms. Gale Gordon died a couple of years later from a broken heart. Relief filled the heart of Warden Verdana after hearing the news. They had committed murder, like the times before and were free to do it again.

Three years passed since the closing of the Northville Prison. Prison overcrowding troubled the State of Florida and the 2001 state prison budget hadn't changed much since 1998.

Overcrowding of the state prisons became top priority in the Governor's office. On July 17, 2001, the Governor and his advisors held a meeting to discuss how they would reduce the overcrowding of prisons.

Money to build additional prisons was not in the budget and the Governor realized it. Alternate solutions were discussed and finally a proposal had been reached. An abandoned prison, particularly the Northville Prison would be renovated.

"This would cut the cost of building a new prison by fifty percent," the Chief Advisor stated, handing a photo of Northville Prison to the Governor.

"Who would be the Warden at this prison," the Governor asked.

"It would be Warden Verdana, who's running a small prison in Texas as we speak. He was once the Warden at Northville Prison and would like to return. He requests that his old guards be reassigned to Northville," the advisor answered. The Governor felt that Verdana's years there made him familiar with the prison and the town, so the Governor agreed, but with one stipulation. He ordered the inmates of the old Northville be transferred back to the new renovated Northville Prison, since the warden housed them in the past.

At the end of the meeting the Governor wanted to know the estimated completion date of the Northville Prison. His Chief Advisor, Charles Pontoon had already began the preparations and only needed his signature.

"The prison will be ready for population on January 1, 2002, and 300 new convicts and 300 of the old convicts of the old Northville Prison would occupy the prison," the Chief Advisor clarified.

"Well done, Charles," the Governor stated, signing his name on the dotted line.

Chapter 5

Back at the prison, the old boiler room had not been included on the list for repairs or replacement during renovations. They built a new heating system in a different location in the prison and locked up the boiler room. The full moon seemed to rest on a congregation of clouds, which lingered above a mountain peak bordering the town.

This particular night the second shift construction workers worked above the boiler room. While using their heavy equipment, movement in the boiler room started. The rats that canvassed the dark tunnel weren't the only things alive. Death was being disturbed.

Dust fell from the ceiling of the boiler room. The light from the light poles in the court yard emanated through a window in the boiler room. Casting a small light in the middle of the dust covered floor on top of a small bible. The bible left behind by Daniel on his journey to the fiery abyss.

Suddenly, the furnace ignited and a conflagration of flames appeared on the floor and danced around the bible. Then, wind blew from the mouth of the boiler, as if someone was breathing, levitating the bible in the air.

The wind subsided and the bible dropped to the floor and the pages turned on their own, stopping suddenly at Psalms 12:1. It read: "In a blink of an eye," and mysteriously a red line of blood appeared under the words.

The pages flipped to the inside cover of the bible revealing Daniel's name he had written there three years earlier.

Abruptly, a complete silence subdued the boiler room and then a loud roar rumbled through the tunnel, leaving a mist of cold grayish fog flowing through the tunnel from Daniel's cold and tormented spirit.

Workers felt the vibrations from the roar and without warning cracks formed in the outside walls of the prison, making a dividing line from the jail cell windows to the ground. Dropping their basic tools the workers also left their machines running, and departed the scene of damnation.

Ron, the construction manager grabbed his cell phone and called the Warden. The conversation was to the point, however; the Warden did not believe Ron.

"The prison's renovation shall and will meet the opening deadline. Obtain new men and fire those who left," the Warden yelled. Ron hesitated looking at the wall, then thought about being paid, shook his head, and then replied.

"I will Warden."

Unknown to Ron, down below in the tunnel inside the fog stood the body of Daniel Gordon with eyes as red as inflamed cinders standing motionless as the fog cleared with four legged rodents walking around him in a circle. He dropped his head and in seconds he disappeared like smoke into the walls and into Northville Prison's reality.

January 1, 2002, the morning of the New Year, the scene was set and the Northville Prison was habitable for the second time. Swarms of onlookers from the town lined up on the other side of the prison's gates. Camera men and women ready to report the opening stood ready. Political speeches were given by the Governor, his advisors, and the Warden at the podium.

"Warden Verdana, any commit on the accusations made four years ago by Daniel Gordon, an inmate of yours about the corruption that went on in

Northville Prison, as well as the accusation by the mother of Daniel Gordon. Implying that you had a hand in her son's disappearance," a news anchor asked.

"Daniel Gordon was never at this prison," the Warden insisted.

Interrupted by the sounds of prison buses pulling up to the prison Warden Verdana lowered his head to the mike, "Sorry, that other question would have to be answered at a later date. I must depart and go to work." Fourteen buses, all in a line brought the six hundred convicts to their new home. After awhile the crowd of spectators slowly diminished.

The last two inmates to exit the bus were Ronald Grimms, the Northville Prison veteran and young Derrick Samuel, a truly innocent man who was incarcerated just weeks ago for allegedly committing an armed robbery at a convenient store. Shackled together by the wrist and by the feet they walked in. Grimms raised his head and stared at the prison in which he lost a dear friend.

"Come on old man, keep moving," Derrick pleaded.

"What's the rush young blood, this prison isn't going anywhere," Grimms replied. The convicts were lined up in the court yard and the guards were positioned in the towers with weapons drown bringing reality to the forgetful. Warden Verdana marched around checking his new arrivals. Then, he stopped in front of Derrick Samuel, who was staring him in the face.

"Oh, you like to stare me down convict?" Verdana asked.

"No Warden," Derrick answered.

"Chief Welsh put this inmate in D-25; place him in D-25. It looks like we might have another feisty one," Verdana yelled, pointing his finger in the eyeball of Derrick.

"Yes sir, Warden," Welsh answered.

"You are going to have to learn to survive in here young blood," Grimms stated, whispering in Derrick's ear.

"I should not be here I didn't commit any crime."

"Well, you are here my friend," Grimms stated.

Chapter 6

Six hundred inmates turned the corner leading to the registration building. They were all amazed by the long crack along the wall of the cell blocks. One of the humorous inmates yelled out, "Warden, I thought this prison was newly renovated. It looks like you missed a spot." The Warden's face turned pale with anger looking at the cracks embedded in his perfect prison.

The outspoken comical inmate spent his first week in the hole for speaking to the Warden without permission.

Warden Verdana made the guards move them all into the building, forming a line at the tables. The inmate's chains were removed and placed in a pile in the center of the room. Identification numbers and housing numbers were called out. Their prison issued clothing and hygiene material were administered.

The morning's beauty dwindled away into the night before they were situated in their cells. They placed Ronald Grimms three cells down from his old cell four years earlier.

Inmate Derrick Samuel walked to D-25; Daniel Gordon's old cell making himself comfortable sitting on his bunk peering out on the tier at passing inmates. His cell was rather bland in color. It had an old wood book shelf that hung to the north of his cell bars about six feet from the floor. The toilet shined of muddy fungus and a roll of toilet paper black in color rested on the edge of the sink. Roaches marched along the cell floor in unison, unafraid of man or death. Above the sink rested a cracked mirror that blurred his image.

"How's it going young blood?" Grimms asked, appearing at the cell bars.

"Well, old man I'm locked up in an eight by ten cell with you standing here, instead of a woman. It's not going so well," Derrick replied.

Grimms walked in slowly as the remembrance of Daniel's demise blurred his vision.

"This cell housed a friend of mine, four years ago. In his life he had done some bad things, but he was a good man and a good friend. Sometimes, prison can change you for the better instead of the worst. De, that's what I called him tried to make it better for the inmates."

"What happened to him?"

"This I don't know, and if I did I could not say," Grimms answered, softly.

"You are a strange old man Grimms," Derrick stated.

"I'd better be going; it will be lights out soon."

"Why didn't you try to find out what happened to him? He was your friend."

Grimms stepped back to the cell's entrance and replied, "I was scared young blood, I was scared," fading away down the tier.

"Lights out!" a tier guard yelled.

The lights slowly flickered as the cell bolts locking emanated through the tier. Footsteps of the guards echoed back to their post. Derrick's panicking thoughts materializing sporadically and faded slowly. He was unaware that soon there would be a *"Ghost in his cell."*

Quietness filled his cell, as he tossed and turned in dire need of his own bed and pillow.

Chapter 7

Derrick sat up on the edge of his bunk with his head down and eyes closed.

Suddenly, unaware a figure appeared in front of him on the other bunk. He opened his eyes with his head down and noticed boots. Slowly, Derrick raised his head and in front of him was a poltergeist making him catapulting from his bunk into the wall by the toilet.

"Why are you in my cell?" the figure spoke, drawing closer to Derrick with a succession of vapors trailing it. Raising its arm the figure pointed to something engraved in the wall. Derrick turned his head with uncertainty, but the darkness concealed it.

He turned back to confront the ghostly figure but it was gone. Slithering down the wall Derrick settled with knees bent on the cold floor. After a few minutes he rose, reached in his pocket, and pulled out a pack of matches...striking one. He canvassed the cell to make sure the figure had departed. The match flickered away so Derrick struck another moving closer to the wall the ghost pointed too. On the wall etched was the name, "Daniel Gordon."

In front of the name Daniel and in back of the name Gordon were crosses and underneath the entire name was the year 1998, along with the words, "I love you mom," with a heart around it.

Soon, the second match dwindled down slightly burning his finger and Derrick struck another one and the ghost appeared in front of him and said, "I shall remember you," walking away through the cell bars turning into a foggy mist evaporating in to the air.

"There's a *Ghost in my Cell,* somebody help me," Derrick yelled. Responding guards ran up the tier stairs to the cell, while inmates yelled, "Be quiet sissy." Arriving at the cell the guards witnessed Derrick in the corner shaking profusely.

"Samuel, what the fuck is the problem? Did you say you saw a ghost?" the guard asked.

"There's a *Ghost in my cell,*" Derrick answered.

"One more out burst like this you little pussy, you're going to the hole," the chief guard explained.

"Everything all right sir," the chief guard's radio squawked.

"Yes, just D-25 being a little bitch talking about a Ghost," the chief guard answered.

"Samuel, you are a newcomer to the prison so you better get with the program or you may just get what the last occupant got," the guard stated, humorously.

Ronald Grimms listened knowing that the ghost Derrick witnessed was Daniel Gordon. Derrick situated himself in the corner of his cell when the guards left until he fell asleep. Eventually, Grimms walked back to his bunk to lie down.

Suddenly, inside Grimms cell a ghostly figure whisked pass his bunk, stopping at the cell bars, hovering for a moment.

"De is that you?" Grimms asked, rising.

"The De you once knew no longer lives, this place is condemned," Daniel's ghost spoke, angrily and then, disappeared. Grimms, a scintillated man laid his head back, placed his head in his hands, and laid there until morning.

Derrick Samuel awoke just in time for roll call. His cell bars opened and his identification number was called. Derrick jumped up, ran to the outside of his cell and stood heroically in line.

"Prisoner 42369!"

"Here!"

"Prisoner 42369, are you the one with the ghost?" the guard asked.

Derrick looked down the line in both directions before he gave an answer. The other inmates where laughing and licking there lips. Finally, Derrick responded, "No that was not me."

"Whatever you say convict," the guard replied.

All inmates had prison employment and Derrick's job consisted of mopping the tier floors everyday.

Roll call ended approximately thirty minutes before chow.

The showers were packed, as Derrick waited for the next open shower head. Grimms with a towel around his waist stood at the mirror shaving his head ball.

Some inmates liked picking on the weak. So as Derrick stood waiting for his turn for an open shower, four inmates from the old Northville approached him.

"You boy, we sure do like the sensitive type," one of the inmates stated. Grimms turned around and said, "Leave the new boy alone."

This has nothing to do with you, Grimms.

"Well, it does now," Grimms replied.

Eventually, they turned to Derrick and one of

them spoke, "Next time when your girlfriend is not around." Derrick's heart palpitations subsided and the fear in his eyes dissipated as they walked away.

"Thanks," looking at Grimms as he stepped into the shower.

"No problem young blood, anytime," Grimms replied. Grimms turned back to finish shaving.

"So you actually saw a ghost in your cell?" Grimms asked. Derrick cleared the soap away from his eyes and

replied, "It was so real."

"It was authentic young blood, I saw him too," Grimms replied.

"You saw him too," Derrick repeated.

"Yes, I saw De, I mean Daniel Gordon," Grimms answered.

The conversation between them ended with both of them thinking about Daniel Gordon. Grimms left Derrick in the washroom, went to dress, and headed to the mess hall.

Chapter 8

The line in the mess hall moved smoothly as usual, when Derrick arrived. Grimms had arrived ten minutes before Derrick. Grimms beckoned Derrick to come over with a quick hand jester while Derrick stood in line. Derrick acquired his plate of Southern goodies and walked over to Grimms.

Following a short spoon and fork frolic with their food, Grimms spoke, "They killed him." Bewildered by the statement by Grimms, Derrick answered with confusion, "They killed who Grimms?"

"The ghost, Daniel Gordon that's who," Grimms replied.

"I don't believe in ghost Grimms, last night was just a hallucination," Derrick stated.

"This morning you said it was so real," Grimms stated.

"I know I did, but hallucinations can be real or at least feel real," Derrick answered. Grimms slammed his fist down on the mess hall table in frustration. Derrick rose from his seat and hollered, "Chill old man, it's my ghost not yours and if you cared so much for him you would have helped this Daniel Gordon four years ago."

One of the corrupt guards over heard the name Daniel Gordon mentioned and immediately, stepped away from his post to inform the Chief of the guards. Derrick walked off and suddenly something whisked pass his ear, leaving an evil feeling in his soul making him stop to look around. After a few minutes he proceeded to the garbage can.

At the garbage can the same feeling in his soul resurfaced leaving the words "In my cell, "in his ear.

Standing there Derrick trembled until his fork and spoon fell off the tray on to the floor. The clamor excited everyone's. Soon, Derrick snapped out of his fright and rotated his body one hundred and eighty degrees placing the other inmates as the audience.

"What's wrong did you see a ghost?" the inmates spoke in unison. Grimms did not join in.

Suddenly, the clock on the south wall struck 10:00 o'clock on the dot and the loud sound through the intercom system made everyone grab their ears. It was Daniel Gordon. However, everyone believed it was a malfunction with the intercom system. Once the demonstration of Daniel's power faded, Derrick discarded his tray and went to work mopping the floors on the tier.

Grimms lingering at the table caught a glimpse of the ghost inside the glass window near him. Grimms couldn't understand why they were the only ones who could see the ghost. Sitting there petrified while gazing at the face of death.

Chapter 9

The Chief of the guards received the news about the two inmates mentioning the name Daniel Gordon. But he wanted to gather all the correct information before he revealed it to the Warden.

Meanwhile, Derrick caressed the white bearded stick as he moved it across the floor of his tier. Everything was tranquil for him, humming the song Angela Bound made by the Neville brothers his father used to sing to him when he was a kid.

Suddenly, Derrick's body became possessed by the ghost, which made him stop mopping and stare off into space. As this terrible thing happened, a guard from the old Northville named Smith approached Derrick.

"Get to mopping convict before I have to give you one right across the head," Smith stated. Derrick's head rose and began staring at the guard, almost as if he was looking straight through him. Smith swallowed with a meager sense of fear and then warned him again about mopping. After no response, Smith began to ease his baton from his side, but Grimms intervened.

"Derrick!" snapping him out of the trance he was in.

"Getting back to mopping boss, getting back to mopping," Derrick yelled. Officer Smith chewed his tongue on both sides, eager for an altercation. Derrick eyes never raised to look upon Smith as he stood there. Eventually, Smith gathered his frustrations together and turned to walk away.

Suddenly, Derrick's spoke, but no one could hear what he was saying except for Smith. The words, "I shall remember you," rang softly on Smith's ear making him turn slowly with flashes of the murder of Daniel Gordon flooding his cerebrum. He could not handle the visions of the blow by blow he administered to Daniel. Smith fell to the floor with his hands covering his face.

"Make it go away, make it go away," Smith screamed. Derrick stood in perfect bliss watching as theguards mind was ripped apart. All the inmates stopped to check out what was happening, circling around the guard. The other guards ran to assist him watching as the guard screamed for dear life.

Suddenly, as everyone looked on, the guard stopped screaming, stopped shaking, and removed his hands from his face.

"Are you all right Smith?" one of the guards asked.

"I'm cool," Smith replied, in a well exhausted voice.

Surprising, to everyone his shakes returned scaring the guard that was helping him up. While this was going on, Derrick continued to mop the floor as he stood on the outside of the circle all alone.

Inside the mop bucket floating on top of the water was the ghostly image of Daniel. Suddenly, Smith's heart began to beat faster and faster. The bruises he administered to Daniel years ago began to appear under his clothes not visible to the on-lookers. With every blow he gave Daniel, his own body flinched with pain.

"I shall remember you," Smith screamed. His eyeballs turned black and he fell dead on the floor. The inmates moved quickly without the leadership of a guard back to their cells. Smith laid there on the cold icy floor, as Derrick continued to mopping and the guards continued to look at their fallen brother waiting for the Warden to come down from his office.

"Let me through, let me through," the Warden screamed. The guards parted like the red sea to let the Warden behold the death of one of their own.

"Well, pick him up and take him to the infirmary," the Warden spoke.

Walking away the Warden happened to notice that Derrick was still mopping in the midst of all the chaos. Derrick raised his head and their eyes met for a brief moment then dropped his head and continued to mop. The Warden fixed his clothes and continued on his way a bit unnerved.

Suddenly, the Warden felt eyes on him and turned in the direction of the feeling. Again, it was Derrick speaking the words, "I shall remember you." The Warden turned and walked off the tier.

Derrick fell into another brain freeze and in a few seconds the ghost left Derrick's body. He looked around and at the top of the tier stood Grimms leaning over the railing.

"What happened Grimms?" Derrick asked.

"You were there, you should know what happened Derrick," Grimms replied.

"It looks like one of the guards died or something,"

Derrick explained.

"It sure seems that way," Grimms replied.

Chapter 10

The entire day the tier stayed empty because everyone was on lock down. Smith's body had to stay in the infirmary until a doctor from the States Coroners Office could be sent out. The death of a guard without any contact from an inmate would have some legal repercussions.

That evening, all the inmates seemed to think about what had happened. Except for Derrick Samuel, who sat whistling in his cell lying back on his bunk; his legs crossed with his arms behind his head, his eyes pearly white with a combination of vermilion in them, and a blackish haze hovered above his berth. Daniel's ghost had not left; he was still extremely alive in Derrick.

Around 9:00 in the next morning as the States Coroner drove through the gates of Northville Prison. Warden Verdana waited patiently out front as the coroner's car pulled up to a halt. The coroner, a plump average height man with sort of a sun tan burnt complexion exited the vehicle. His two-tone rust and black bag lingered on his side full of his medical equipment.

"Good morning, Dr. Stans," the Warden spoke, extending his hand of friendship.

"What's good about it Warden," the Coroner replied, reaching out to shake the Warden's hand.

"The prison hasn't been open a week and it's all ready a death, a freaking guard for crying out loud. There are a lot of people very nervous about this. Especially, the Governor who gave you this job," Dr. Stans stated.

"Don't worry, it was just a freak accident, I believe Mr. Smith had some medical problems."

"Warden Verdana, I'm surprise," Stans stated.

"Surprised about what?" Verdana asked.

"I'm surprised that you actually know the names of your employees," Dr. Stans replied.

"Well, this particular guard was with me four years ago at the old Northville," the Warden answered.

"Well, lead the way to the body," Dr. Stans ordered.

"Right this way sir, I've cleared the entire morgue of its personnel as a precautionary measure," the Warden stated, as they entered the morgue.

Chrome carts where shining, the floors were immaculate, and in the center on a table lay the dead body of Mr. Smith tucked away under a white sheet. Dr. Stans loosened his tie, retrieved the tools of his trade from his bag, put on his old medical robe, and slid his hands into some rubber gloves.

"Let's get started," Dr. Stans spoke, adjusting his glasses.

Very slowly, Dr. Stans pulled the sheet off the body of the guard dropping it on the floor and started removing the clothing. He unbuttoned the shirt of the guard and there were numerous bruises like footprints and whelps covering his chest. Their eyes grew large with uncertainty, panicking as the doctor removed the guard's pants witnessing more bruises. Smith's entire body looked as if he was beaten to death. With reservation in his eyes Dr. Stans turned to the Warden.

"What the hell is going on here Warden?" Dr. Stans asked, nervously. Warden Verdana's vocal cords must have taken a break, because he could not reply. He just stared at the brutalized body of his guard. Dr. Stans continued his autopsy as the Warden stood there motionless. His hands moving down the guard's body checking for anything else unusual.

Quickly, Dr. Stans hands sprung from the chest of the guard, and by this time the Warden had awoke from his inaudible state.

"What now?" the Warden asked, stuttering.

"This mans ribs are broken, I mean all of his ribs are broken," Dr. Stans explained. Dr. Stans fell back into a chair that was stationed next to the table. His hands shaking perfuse, retrieving a cigarette out of his shirt pocket puffing frantically, as he stared at the body.

"Stans, Dr. Stans are you all right?" the Warden asked.

Suddenly, the lights went off inside the morgue and neither of them could see each other. When the lights came on Dr. Stans rose from his chair while the Warden peered down at the body with astonishment. The marks of a badly bruised and beaten guard existed know more. Even his ribs after being examined again by Dr. Stans were intact. The stage was set for, "Terror."

"This concludes my autopsy," Stans stated, in a state of shock.

"There's some strange shit going on in your prison Warden, something really strange," Dr. Stans expressed, gathering his things leaving the Warden next to the dead body.

"Just keep this between us Stans," the Warden bellowed, before Stans reached the morgue doors. Dr. Stans stopped, peered back at the Warden and said, "No one would believe me if I told them." Warden Verdana picked up the white sheet off the floor and began covering the guard up.

Suddenly, he noticed that the bruises and whelps that vanished earlier had returned. He quickly threw the sheet over the guard and pushed the table into the corner of the room. Smith's body fell to the floor on impact and the Warden backed away with confusion, slamming the door and locking it until the guards family could be notified of the accident.

Behind the locked doors of the morgue the bruises on Smith's body disappeared again.

Chapter 11

As the coroner drove out of the prison, Derrick stood in his cell window watching with a smirk on his face. Suddenly, Derrick's forearm muscles began to pulsate and his entire body jerked. Daniel was finally leaving his body. This possession left Derrick very weak and with a false sense of security as he regained splashed water on his face.

The tier was very active that morning. Inmates were roaming the floors, and talking about what had happened the day before. Derrick put on a clean tee shirt and prepared himself for his daily mopping duty. Warden Verdana sat in his office thinking about what had happened in the infirmary that morning. Chief Welsh walked in interrupting his deep thought startling the Warden.

"Warden Verdana sir, the ambulance is here to pick up Smith," Welsh spoke.

"Very well Chief see to it that they have everything they need," the Warden replied. Chief

Welsh turned to walk away when Warden Verdana spoke, "Chief, do you think anything is going on in the prison that's unusual?"

"No sir," Welsh replied.

"How about any inmates that seem to be acting strange?" the Warden asked, while tapping his ink pen on his desk.

"No sir," Welsh answered.

"If you see or hear anything unusual bring it to my attention ASAP," the Warden ordered.

"Yes sir, Warden," Welsh spoke, nodding his head.

Now, the scene on the tier and in the entire prison was the same as the day before. Grimms had made his way from his cell to Derrick's cell before he left for his duty.

"Young blood, how are you doing today?" Grimms asked, with his back leaning against the cell bars.

"I feel just like I did yesterday, pissed off about being in here when I'm an innocent man," Derrick replied.

"Young blood, I believe we have a ghost in this prison and its name is Daniel Gordon," Grimms stated.

"How many times do I have to tell you I do not believe in apparitions? Excuse me," Derrick stated, pissed off moving pass Grimms. Grimms extended his arm and placed his hand on Derrick's shoulder and said, "Young blood you are going to need a friend in here."

"You mean the same kind of friend you were to Daniel. No, thank you, I'll rather foot it alone," Derrick replied. Grimms hand dropped to his side and Derrick proceeded to his duty, leaving Grimms pondering.

Derrick reached the bottom of the steps and two guards from the old Northville Prison who was part of the murder cover up stood in his way. Instead of waiting for them to move, Derrick blew through them like they weren't there, infuriating them. The guards calmed themselves. However, the other inmates that were part of the old Northville couldn't wait to get a piece of the young Derrick Samuel.

Chapter 12

Derrick started mopping his portion of the tier. Then, the guard from the earlier incident approached him insisting that he gather more mopping solution from the store room. Unaware that he was being set up for a beating, as the guard escorted him to a fairly small store room with only one way in or out. The guard let Derrick walk in first to pick up the gallon of solution by the shelf on the east wall.

Suddenly, another guard stepped out from behind the shelf on the west wall and struck him with a baton. Instantly, the other guard joined in. Both beating him for about ten minutes until the store room door swung open and Chief Welsh stood in the doorway. Timing was on Derrick's side because if Welsh hadn't walked in, Derrick would have definitely died.

"That's enough," the Chief stated, in a calm voice.

"Take him to the infirmary and get back on your job," the Chief continued.

"Sir he's a strange person, he just pushed through us as we stood by the steps. No inmate has every intentionally done this, but he did it on purpose," one of the guards explained.

"I will not inform the Warden," the Chief replied.

Back at the tier, while playing cards Grimms noticed that Derrick had not returned. Grimms through his hand in and proceeded to find Derrick. As Grimms turned the corner down the hall he noticed two guards placing Derrick on a stretcher unconscious with a bloody face.

Quickly, Grimms hide on the side of the wall as they walked pass him.

Grimms turned to creep back to the tier, but in front of him appeared an inmate from the old Northville Prison. Isaac Matthew, a convict serving two consecutive life sentences and the leader of the inmate crew who worked for the Warden.

"Something over here for you to see," Matthew stated, angrily.

"No, I was just looking for my friend," Grimms replied, nervously.

"Did you find him?" Matthew asked.

"No," Grimms replied, walking away towards the tier. Matthew watched as he squirmed away like a little bitch. Laughing at him out loud so everyone on the tier would hear.

Back, in the infirmary the prison doctors worked long into the night, wrapping and slinging, while monitoring Derrick. They concluded about 9:00 pm.

Around 10:00 pm all the doctors and nurses left for the night. Derrick was left alone, except for a guard on the outside of the infirmary and another inmate next to him.

Derrick regained consciousness around 11:00 pm, locked down by the bed restraints. The night's moon glowing as he gazed at it.

Suddenly, the prison break alarm sounded. The yard lights activated; the sirens rang loudly, the guards were scrambling, the tier lights blinked red for alert, and the inmates stood at their cell bars.

Through the sounds of the sirens the inmates shouted, "Who is it, who is trying to escape?" Warden Verdana rose from his fold-out bed as Chief Welsh phoned him from the guard tower at the entrance to the prison.

"Sir, it's a escape attempt," Welsh stated.

"Who was it, one of the new convicts?" the Warden asked.

"No sir, it was actually Ferguson," Welsh replied.

"You mean one of our loyal inmates," the Warden asked, curiously.

"Yes sir, we spotted him running across the yard attempting to reach the South gate to climb it. After numerous warnings to stop, he wouldn't. He wasn't himself. He just kept trying to climb. We fired hitting him at least twenty to thirty times until he finally dropped to the ground. There was something strange about him," Welsh explained.

"What was it?" the Warden asked.

"When he fell to the ground I swear I witnessed a light float from his body like a spirit or something. Our guards from the old Northville witnesses it also. I know because I asked them individually," Welsh replied.

"He probably touched the electrical wire before he fell," the Warden explained.

"You're probably right sir, you just told me to let you know of anything strange," Chief Welsh stated. Warden Verdana hung the phone up, walked over to the window, and stared out of it.

"Why would anyone try to get over the gate when they know that at the top of it there are electrical wires with 20,000 volts running through them?" the Warden thought. He shrugged his shoulders and walked over to his bed and went back to sleep.

Chapter 13

The Wardens was interrupted again after only thirty minutes, but not by Chief Welsh or an escape attempt. The touch of death woke him in the form of a nightmare with sweat running down his face making him sit up on the edge of his bed with his feet dangling. He felt and smelled a presence of some kind as he leaned over and turned on the small table lamp. But there was nothing.

Paranoia settled into the deepest part of his cruel soul. His eyes panned around his office, trying to find some kind of rational explanation for it all.

After a few seconds the Warden decided to leave the somberness of his bed to walk over to his door. His left foot touched the floor first, but it didn't feel like his plush carpet he had laid during the new renovation. He looked down and under his feet were hot cinders cascading over his office floor. Inching closer and closer to the door, the further it seemed. As he reached for the door knob like an inexperienced paratrooper reaching for the ground.

Suddenly, the door shrunk in size until it disappeared. The ceiling began to crumble, dropping pieces of plaster down on him knocking him unconscious. Strange things began happening in his office while he was unconscious. Hell's gate opened up and Daniel Gordon peeped out of the gate to spy on the Warden's soul.

In the morning, the Warden awoke rising to inventory his office. He ran to the door to check it and when he opened it Ms. Castile sat at here desk on the phone.

"Good morning Warden, slept in last night. You look a little tired. Did you get enough sleep last night?" Ms. Castile asked. Warden Verdana backed his head from out of the door, closed it, and walked the floor saying, "It was just a dream, just a dream."

Suddenly, Ms. Castile phone rung.

"Sir, the Governor is on the phone," Ms. Castile stated.

Back in the infirmary Derrick was recovering very well, receiving some needed rest. The doctors told him he would be able to go back to population the next day. This made Derrick feel good. He was tired of being in the house of death, as his father use to call it. In the bed across from Derrick, an inmate explained that he fell down some stairs after seeing something glide pass him. During the early part of Derrick's stay in the infirmary the inmate was kept sedated.

Around dusk, back on the tier, uneasiness touched everyone because of the recent deaths in the prison. These earlier incidents were warm-ups to more of Daniel's terror. Death to the innocent who stands in his way and death to the ones whose cruel acts of violence made him, *"EVIL."*

Chapter 14

Deeds, one of the corrupt guards made his rounds. Deeds, was a real hard ass, a former police officer on the outside until changed with excessive force. Deeds proceeded down the corridor that connected the Aids ward with the counselor's office and administrative offices whistling a verse from the battle hymn republic, as he turned the corner towards the gun room.

Suddenly, Deeds screamed and then there was a gun shot. Guards advanced from every direction to the scene finding Deeds laying face down on the floor with a shot gun in his left hand. Even though, he was a right hander. The guards stood there in a state of shock. Warden Verdana heard about the gun shot over the radio. The Chief ordered the guards to turn Deeds over. Deeds face had been completely blown away and his right finger pointed towards the artillery room.

"What the hell is going on?" the Warden asked, angrily, arriving late.

"Hell is right," the Chief replied.

"Where did he get a shot gun from?" the Warden asked.

"The artillery room sir," the Chief spoke.

"I know that we have guns in the artillery room, but why did Deeds have one," the Warden asked. One guard took it upon himself to visit the artillery room. Looking through the partially opened door the guard noticed something on the floor he believed to be blood.

"Chief!" the guard yelled.

"What is it?" Chief Welsh asked, in a loud voice. The guard curved his arm slowly, gesturing the Chief and the Warden to come see. Chief Welsh propelled the door open and in full site were the words, "I shall remember you," written in blood…Deeds' blood.

Suddenly, the images of the heinous crime they committed four years earlier haunted their souls.

"Sir's are you both all right?" one of the guards asked. Welsh turned and said, "Get somebody to clean this up and move Deeds body to the morgue."

Out of the blue, a loud yell emanated from one of the guards still standing over Deeds.

"Warden Sir, his shot gun is not loaded and hasn't been fired," a guard stated.

"Hand the shot gun to me," the Warden ordered. He inspected the shot gun and his facial expression changed quickly from curious to afraid.

It took awhile to get the body of Deeds to the morgue traveling pass the infirmary where Derrick laid in peace. The sound of the bed being rolled through the corridor made Derrick rise to see where it was coming from.

"You guard. Who is the lucky contestant?"

Derrick asked, jokingly. Frustration aligned their faces, as they rolled another one of their own to the morgue within a week.

Rumors began spreading about another guard's death making the inmates become nervous and unsteady. Grimms spoke out about the problem; telling everyone about the ghost in the prison. Everyone laughed at old Grimms, telling him to leave those drugs alone. Unwarranted, Grimms words were over heard by one on the prison guards from the old Northville. The guard notified Chief Welsh and Chief Welsh notified the Warden.

That evening, Chief Welsh visited Grimms in his cell.

"So you are the one spreading these rumors about a Ghost?" the Chief asked.

"Yes sir, I believe there is a ghost here," Grimms answered, nervously.

"Well convict, the Warden wants a few words with you," Welsh stated. As the Chief lead Grimms through the tier to the Warden's office. Sounds of snickering and jokes emanated from the other inmates.

"Ghost man, call the ghost busters!" different inmates yelled.

"Well, Grimms it looks like you have a lot of people who believe you," the Chief stated, humorously. Soon, the news of Grimms' ghost reached Derrick in the infirmary.

"That crazy old man, told everyone that there's a ghost in here," Derrick spoke, talking to the inmate that lay across from him.

Now, in the Warden's office Grimms sat while the Warden stared out of his window.

"So Grimms, you say there's a ghost in the prison," the Warden asked.

"Yes sir."

"Who's the ghost?" the Warden asked.

"It is my friend, Daniel Gordon," Grimms replied.

"Daniel Gordon you say," the Warden repeated.

"If you don't believe me ask Derrick Samuel the one that's in Daniel's old cell," Grimms replied.

"I will, but don't say anything else about a ghost," the Warden asked.

"Yes Warden," Grimms replied.

"You can leave now," the Warden ordered, as Chief Welsh walked Grimms out.

"Welsh bring Samuel to me immediately," the Warden ordered, before Welsh reached the doorway.

"Yes sir," Welsh answered. Grimms walked back to the tier without an escort and went to his cell, wondering if telling the Warden about Daniel's ghost was the right thing to do.

Chapter 15

Around five o' clock Chief Welsh entered the infirmary.

"Samuel, get up, the Warden wants to see you," Welsh stated.

"For what?" Derrick asked.

"Don't worry about it, just get up." Derrick rose, gathered his things.

"Derrick Samuel," the Warden stated, as Derrick walked in.

"Have a seat son. Now, I understand that you know about a ghost in my prison, a certain Daniel Gordon to be more specific," the Warden continued.

"No sir, I don't believe in ghost."

"Well, your friend Grimms said different."

"Grimms Sir, Grimms is an old man with half a mind," Derrick replied.

"Really, this is all Samuel. You can go back to your cell early," the Warden insisted. Derrick walked back to the tier catching the eyes of all the inmates. He proceeded up the stairs about to pass Grimms' cell but paused and stared with glowing eyes at Grimms. He had become possessed by Daniel's ghost again.

"Foolish old man," the ghost spoke. Grimms slammed back into his wall staring into the eyes of evil.

Soon, Derrick's eyes cleared and he walked away. Grimms had never been that scared in his life as he inched to his cell bars and watched Derrick, walk to his cell.

Meanwhile, in the office, Warden Verdana unlocked a desk drawer and grabbed a disk and inserted it into his computer. After hitting a few keys Daniel Gordon's file uploaded. Staring at the face of Daniel Gordon, the Warden plummeted into deep thought, while a storm brewed outside.

Lightning struck the prison's power supply, causing a blackout interrupting his train of thought.

"Lock down, lock down!"

The inmates became unnerved by the blackout, trying to return to their cells before the bars automatically closed. Grimms arrived at his cell from the television area just before his cell bars closed. In his cell Derrick was acting strange standing in the middle of his cell, not moving, with the skin on his face rolling like waves.

Suddenly, Daniel's ghost manifested from out of the shell of Derrick making its way to Grimms' cell. Grimms, unaware that this would be the last breathe he would take. Daniel's ghost unseen by the other inmates floated down the walk way, arriving at Grimms' cell. Grimms rested on the toilet when the entity appeared in front of him. Slowly, Grimms rose and the entity spoke, "You were supposed to be my friend."

"Wait, wait, Daniel, I'm your friend," Grimms replied.

"A friend in deed I do not need," Daniel stated. Then, he blew a greenish fog from his mouth. The fog covered the entire cell in the form of an air tight chamber stopping the air from getting in and sound getting out, like a decompression chamber on space ships. Grimms screamed while holding his chest struggling for air then fell to the floor.

Blood started to flow from his eyes and his head began to pulsate then exploded, leaving a headless man lying dead in his cell. Daniel's ghost stood motionless gazing at the corpse of Grimms. Daniel faded away into oblivion when the lights in the prison switched on. The guards made their rounds to check on the inmates when they came across Grimms.

"Inmate down, inmate down," a guard screamed.

"What's going on?" the inmates including Derrick yelled, as the guards made their way to Grimms' cell witnessing a form of death unwelcome to the human eye.

"Call the Chief," one of the guards screamed.

Chief Welsh made his way to the cell and couldn't believe his eyes. Frozen with fear the Chief's eyes roamed the cell for evidence, but there was none. Minutes later, the Chief stormed out and walked down the walk way pass Derrick's cell. Derrick grasping his cell bars with his head down seemed to waiting on him. Chief Welsh stopped, turned to Derrick, and stared. Derrick's head rose slowly, then he spoke, "There's a *Ghost in my cell*," jokingly. Chief Welsh pulled his baton out and struck Derrick's cell bars, but Derrick did not flinch. After a few seconds Welsh walked off and grabbed his radio off his side.

"Warden, there has been another death sir."

"Who was it?" the Warden asked.

"Grimms sir, in his locked cell," Chief Welsh replied. Warden Verdana fell back into his chair, clamping his teeth down on his fingers making blood ooze from his finger.

Chapter 16

The next morning the Warden's voice bellowed over the intercom system. "After your daily work assignment you are to report back to your cells for lock down until further notice." The inmates became outraged by the change, but a little grateful. Chief Welsh walked into Warden Verdana's office after being summoned.

"Chief Welsh we need to find out what is going on here," the Warden stated.

"Yes sir, Warden. But do you realized that everyone that is dying had something to do with Daniel Gordon's death," Welsh stated.

"So what are you saying?" the Warden asked.

"I'm saying that we maybe next," Welsh replied.

"Well, Welsh I do not believe in ghost and I need for you to get to the bottom of this," the Warden stated.

"Yes sir," Welsh answered, fearfully. Chief Welsh called his wife to tell her how much he loved her as the Warden received a phone call from a news reporter.

"Good morning Warden, this is Steve Limski from Channel Five News," Mr. Limski spoke.

"What can I do for you?" the Warden asked, clearing his throat.

"Well, Warden we understand it's been some unexplained deaths at your prison."

"I'm sorry but your sources have misinformed you. Good day Mr. Limski," the Warden replied, quickly hanging up the phone.

Back inside population, Derrick had moved up from mop detail to the laundry room. Three inmates plus Derrick had the responsible for the washing. This was a peaceful duty for Derrick; no guards around to bother him, but a place where rapes and beatings could take place.

Now, while Derrick folded a basket of clothes listening to his head phones. He was unaware of the other inmates being waved away by Matthew and his crew. These were the ones who participated in Daniel's death.

Abruptly, his head phones were taken off of his ears by Frankie, one of Matthew's men. Derrick turned around and Matthew, Whitey, Little Tim, Frankie, and Monk with smiles on there faces stood in front of him.

"Derrick, I'm so glad you are here, we need to talk," Matthew stated, licking his lips. His four comrades moved in quickly on Derrick. Subduing him and bending him over the laundry table, Matthew, having first contact.

Derrick struggled until one of his arms was freed striking Monk in his eye. Then, Whitey struck him with an elbow to the back of his head, knocked him to the floor.

"Pick him up," Matthew ordered. Unbeknown to the five rapists, Derrick became possessed as they picked Derrick up. His eyes swelled turning pearly white and they let him go and stepped back. The outraged Matthew shouted, "Kill that motherfucking bitch." As they approached him, the cell bars, the dryer doors, and washing lids started to open and close.

Suddenly, the ghost's said, "I shall remember you." Matthew and his crew froze with fear, as Derrick walked around them making them dizzy. When Derrick stopped in place they all snapped out of it.

"Let's get the fuck out of here," Matthew hollered. They all turned to run, however; only Matthew and Monk escaped. Whitey, Little Tim, and Frankie's feet settled into a floor of quicksand, slowly pulling them down.

"Help us, help us," they screamed. As their bodies sank into the floor the floor hardened back to its original state showing only their heads. The pressure from the hardening floor burst their eyeballs out killing them instantly. Matthew and Monk were able to make it to the bar doors and out of the laundry room. They proceeded through the prison screaming frantically, knocking down inmates in their path.

Before reaching their cell, they ran into Chief Welsh and Warden Verdana standing at the guard desk on the tier. They explained what had happened to them. The Chief radioed for back up to met him in the laundry room. When backup, the Chief, and the Warden walked into the laundry room Derrick's folded clothes with his head phones back on and his back to them. The three men lay dead in the floor with their eyeballs lying in front of them.

They rushed Derrick and subdued him.

"What's the problem Warden?" Derrick asked. Warden Verdana moved to the side from blocking Derrick's line of sight, so he could see the three men in the floor.

"What the fuck, happened to them?" Derrick asked.

"This is what we want to know, you were in here," the Warden stated. Derrick replied, "I had my head phones on all the time, I didn't hear anything.

"Take him to the hole, until I can sort this out," the Warden ordered.

"And them sir," Welsh spoke, pointing to the dead inmates.

"Get the engineers to dig them out," Warden Verdana answered.

Chapter 17

They hog tied Derrick as he screamed he had nothing to do with the inmates getting killed. Wanton, the guard who beat Derrick in the store room to almost extinction helped take Derrick to the hole. Arriving at the hole, they stripped Derrick down to his birthday suit and placed him in. The hole was a stone box about ten feet high with one light brighter than the sun. Derrick had calmed down some what when Wanton walked in and stood in his face.

"You're a lucky one, I should have killed you in the store room," Wanton stated. Derrick began crawling to the corner and Wanton kicked him in his back causing him to hit the wall hard.

"Don't you ever turn your back on me convict," Wanton yelled, as the other guard stood outside. Staring at Derrick for a moment Wanton walked out of the cell, slamming the door behind him. Derrick slid down the wall to the floor in pain with tears flowing down his face.

In the laundry room the engineers were using the jack hammer to break up the cement floor to retrieve the three dead inmates. Warden Verdana watched as the heads of the inmates were struck by the cement pieces propelled from the jack hammer. Chief Welsh walked in and whispered in the ear of the Warden that Derrick Samuel was tucked away in the hole.

"Chief Welsh what is going on here?" Verdana asked, as the engineers hammered.

"I do not know Warden but it's getting to weird and it seems to have something to do with Daniel Gordon," Welsh replied.

"Do you believe in ghost Welsh?" the Warden asked.

"No sir, but I believe that what you reap, you shall sew," Welsh answered. Warden Verdana trudged away out of the room with his arms folded and head down leaving Chief Welsh to supervise the engineers. The Warden headed to the hole to speak with Derrick. Arriving at the cell, Warden Verdana slid open the window on the metal door to see Derrick.

"Samuel, who are you?" the Warden asked. Derrick rose from his corner slowly and walked to the window.

"My name is Derrick Samuel, an inmate like everyone else here at Northville," Derrick answered.

"What do you know about an inmate named Daniel Gordon?" the Warden asked.

"I've never met him, but I understand that he use to reside in my cell some years ago," Derrick replied. While talking, Derrick moved closer to the window and the Warden could see Derrick's eyes beginning to change. Verdana closed the slide window in fear and said, "Derrick you can go back to your cell tomorrow and walked away. Derrick went back to his corner and sat down.

His pearly white eyes showing that Daniel Gordon's ghost had returned.

Without warning, a mist like fog withdrew from his body and there stood Daniel Gordon. Daniel spoke, "In my cell, in a hole behind my mirror there are files that proves the Warden's corruption, along with guards and inmates. But do not get them, I have not finished yet."

"Why can't you get them," Derrick asked, rolling up in a ball with fear. Daniel's ghost replied, "I can not touch them for some reason, I tried. You have to be my initial portal, my starting point for some reason, but not all the time. Some things I can do alone."

"I'm sorry Daniel, I'm sorry they did that to you," Derrick stated.

"They will all pay," Daniel hollered, making the walls shake and evanesced into the floor leaving Derrick speechless and possessed no more.

In the Warden's office Ms. Castile formed a memo stating that all inmate correspondence coming in or going out and phone usage for the time being for inmates would be halted. The Warden was basically shutting down the entire prison until he could get some answers. Ms. Castile had been taking messages for the Warden from the State, all day. They were looking for explanations about the recent murderers.

"Sir, the Governor's office is on the phone again," Ms. Castile stated.

"Tell them I'm not in the office," the Warden ordered.

"Yes sir, Warden," Ms. Castile replied.

Verdana spent around in his chair staring out of the window, seeking a solution to his problem. The only witness to the three inmates dying in the floor, knew nothing about it and could not have done it.

On the tier, Matthew and Monk had spread the word about the three inmates that died in the floor stirring up panic. Matthew and Monk were cell mates sitting in their cell trying to think of away to kill Derrick. While they talked Wanton quietly appeared at their cell bars over hearing them conspiring to kill Derrick.

"You two wouldn't be trying to kill Derrick Samuel would you?" Wanton asked.

"He killed our boys Wanton, you can understand that," Matthew answered.

"Well yes, but he's mine," Wanton spoke.

"Let us help like we did with that Daniel mother fucker?" Monk insisted.

"No, I got this one. I'm on my way down to the hole right now," Wanton explained. Matthew and Monk's face gleamed with happiness as Wanton stepped away, both unaware that Daniel's ghost lye wait in the walls listening to their conversation.

Chapter 18

Meanwhile, Derrick returned his tray through his door to a guard, as Wanton strolled through the prison towards the hole, running into Cummings, a guard that had something to do with Daniel's death and the assault on Derrick.

"Listen here Wanton, I got this girl coming later on tonight. You want in," Cummings asked.

"Hell yeah, about what time," Wanton replied.

"About 11:00 tonight," Cummings answered. They parted ways, Cummings making his way to the guard's locker room and Wanton to the hole. Unknown to Wanton, Daniel's ghost entered through the walls and into Derrick's soul while he rested.

At Derrick's cell door Wanton looked in through the sliding window. Derrick's head was down and he was not moving. Wanton stuck the key in the door and slowly opened it.

"Derrick Samuel. Convict, get ready to die,"

Wanton spoke.

Suddenly, Derrick's head rose with his eyes completely white. The door slammed quickly behind Wanton making him turn towards the door.

But when he turned back around Derrick had disappeared. Wanton surveyed the area looking for Derrick, and fear settled in and he shuffled to the door to open it, but it was locked. Standing there the sliding window opened and Derrick stood looking at Wanton from outside the cell.

"Help me, somebody help me," Wanton screamed.

Suddenly, water began seeping in through the floor edges rising over his boot heel. Wanton attempted to get help by screaming again, but no one came. Rising higher and higher the water had exceeded Wanton's knees and seconds later it had reached his chest overpowering Wanton causing him to float.

Soon, the water reached the ceiling shorting out the light, sending a surge of energy through the entire prison making the lights in the tier flicker on and off.

Now, at his locker Cummings sprayed on some cologne, as the lights flickered.

Wanton had taken his last breath as he tried to

raise his noise up through the small bars at the ceiling. However, he drowned and his dead corpse descended to the floor.

Quickly, the water seceded leaving not a drop on the floor, but Wanton's clothes where soaking wet.

The cell door swung open and Derrick raised his hands and the body of Wanton slid across the floor until it reached the outside of the cell away from the door. Derrick stared at Wanton then walked back into his cell and the door closed behind him leaving Wanton laying in a puddle of water with no water trail from the cell.

Still possessed Derrick lowered himself down on to the dry frigid floor necked and awaited for someone to find Wanton.

Then, a loud roar from Derrick's soul erupted and Daniel's ghost withdrew from his body into the air and vanished.

Monk was on his way to his drug stash hidden away in a vent inside a cell when he stumbled upon Wanton laying in the middle of the corridor by Derrick's door. Quickly, Monk deserted the area without checking Wanton's vitals running into Chief Welsh leaving the tier on his way to lunch.

Out of breath; Monk explained what he had witnessed.

"Code red, Officer down!" Welsh yelled, sprinting off the tier. The Warden, Chief Welsh, Monk, and a few guards arrived at Derrick's cell door.

Chief Welsh eased over to the body first hollering Wanton's name, but no reply. He reached down to check his pulse and shook his head to let everyone know that Wanton was dead. Welsh noticed that Wanton's uniform was wet.

"Warden, Wanton clothes are soaking wet,"
the Chief explained.

"That's impossible, there's no water down here," the Warden replied.

"Come feel him yourself Warden," Welsh asked. The Warden walked over, reached down and touched Wanton's clothes jolting back in fear.

"He's wet, but there's no water on the floor," Verdana stated. Monk, the closest to Derrick's cell heard Derrick moving around so he headed to the door and opened the window. Derrick rested in the corner with his eyes pearly white. Monk yelled in fear pointing to Derrick.

"Step a side Monk," the Warden ordered. When the Warden looked at Derrick's eyes and they where normal.

"Monk, what's the problem, everything seems to be okay with Derrick."

"Derrick, did you hear anything going on out here?" the Warden asked.

"No Sir, Warden," Derrick spoke, in a calm voice. Welsh kneeled down to inspect the body some more and said, "Warden. Wanton's face is purple and there's water in his mouth. It looks like he drowned, sir."

"It's Samuel, something is strange about him, he's the Killer," Monk yelled.

"No, I believe its Daniel Gordon's ghost," the Chief spoke. Warden Verdana looked at Welsh as if he agreed.

"Welsh are you getting spooked or something," Verdana asked.

"No sir, I'm just saying that this was not done by man, that's all," Welsh replied.

"Take him to the morgue," the Warden ordered. When Monk, Welsh, and a guard picked Wanton up there were words, "I SHALL REMEMBER YOU," carved in his chest:

Quickly, they dropped him to the floor and stared. The Warden had already left the scene, so he didn't see it. In a flaccid voice Chief Welsh said, "Pull down his shirt," to the guard.

"Let's go," Welsh ordered.

Chapter 19

Cummings hadn't heard about Wanton's death on his way to the back door to let the prostitute in. Eerie spider webs hung from the ceiling of the corridor to the back door and he was right on schedule.

"Knock, knock." Cummings opened it and there stood a five foot eight woman, with ruby red lips and a figure that strangled a man's lustful mind. She dressed in a hot short black leather skirt that hugged her thighs enhancing the red blouse that showed her cleavage and nipples. Cummings invited her in with a grin on his face and closed the door behind her. They made a quick left down a smaller corridor leading to a small area not to far from the old boarded up tunnel to the boiler room. Cummings couldn't wait; he had been down there earlier to set up a little bed. Arriving Cummings quickly took off his clothing and laid down on the bed. She unzipped her skirt on the side and it dropped to the floor, her blouse had snaps so it came off quickly. Suddenly, she was just as necked as Cummings.

On top of him she climbed to start their pilgrimage to sexual intercourse. While making love they heard noises that didn't derive from them coming from the boarded up tunnel.

Cummings rose, slipped on his pants and asked her to wait until he checked it out.

Slowly, Cummings moved down the corridor until he arrived at the boarded up tunnel leading to the old boiler room. He inspected the boards, the nails and everything seemed to be okay.

Suddenly, he heard noises coming from the other side of the wall of wood, and then heard the back door close.

"Damn she left," Cummings stated, assuming that it was her slamming the door. Cummings fastened his belt and turned back to the wall of wood. Suddenly, he remembered that he left everything back on the bed, including his radio, hoping that the girl didn't take it with her.

Chapter 20

Cummings peeped through the cracks in the wood and without warning the wood began to pulsate, startling him. He slipped and fell backwards on the floor. As the wall pulsated, the image of Daniel formed inside the wood and stepped out of it made of wood. Cummings scooted backwards on the floor trying to get away from the thing.

Suddenly, the wood man transformed into a wood woman with breast and a figure like a real women.

"You like," the ghost stated, as Cummings sat there in fright. The woman reached down and picked Cummings up from off the floor and held him in her arms. She embraced him with a soft woody kiss on the lips, as he tried to struggle. She pulled her lips away from his lips and stared at him with eyes void of substance.

"Please, please Daniel, they made me," Cummings yelled.

The wood figure leaned in for another kiss, but this time it opened its mouth wide like a snake eating their prey and began gobbling down Cummings whole, until the only thing visible were his feet dangling out of her mouth.

In a sudden gulp, Cummings was gone. His body swirled down her throat into her stomach making an indentation that revealed she was stuffed and changed back into Daniel and walked into the wall of wood, reforming with the wood's flat surface again, but with a noticeable bulge. His shirt, baton, and radio were the only things left of him back in a room know one would ever look for him to be.

He had vanished without a trace.

Chapter 21

Hours had elapsed since Cummings dinner date, and no guards seemed to be able to locate him. The Warden had acquired him a weapon from the gun room after finding Wanton dead in the hole. As he loaded it Mr. Charles Albright from the Governor's office stormed into his office. Ms. Castile tried to stop him, but could not.

"Mr. Albright," the Warden spoke, surprised to see him!

"Warden, we've been trying to contact you for the past three day. Now, what is going on here?" Albright asked.

"Take a seat sir; you may not believe this. You see Albright; we have had a few more unexplained deaths' here. Some guards and some inmates," Warden Verdana stated.

"A few is too many, I believe Warden," Albright replied.

"I believe you are right," Verdana stated.

"Unexplained you say," Albright continued.

"Yes," Warden Verdana stated, as Chief Welsh entered the office over hearing their conversation.

"This is Chief Welsh, Mr. Albright."

"We both believe that there may be a ghost involved in these deaths," Welsh stated. Albright turned and Welsh nodded his head.

Turning back to Verdana, Albright spoke, "A ghost, I tell you what Warden Verdana we were going to let you handle this, but since I have heard this. I'm informing you that the prison will be run by another Warden starting next week," Albright stated.

"But there is a ghost in this prison," Verdana replied.

"Why would a ghost want to kill your men and inmates?" Albright asked.

"We don't know, everyone is treated fairly in my prison," the Warden replied.

"Not true. If we go by the accusations made four years ago. We will replace you Warden," Albright stated.

Albright turned to exit, but the office lights began to flicker, the office door closed, and the windows turned to ice. Ms. Castile began banging on the office door trying to get in. The three could actually see the cold smoke coming from their mouths.

"What is going on here Warden?" Albright asked.

"I told you we have a ghost sir," Verdana replied.

Suddenly, while they stood in fear, the Warden's computer turned on by itself making a ringing noise that caught the attention of Albright. Albright walked around the desk and peered at the computer screen. His eyes looked at the docket of Daniel Gordon on the screen. "Warden, four years ago you stated that Daniel Gordon was never here. But this file, states differently. What happened to Daniel Gordon? Warden, we do not need a scandal," Albright spoke.

The Warden started to part his lips to lye, but Chief Welsh's eyes turned pearly white and he spoke, "I shall remember you," then Daniel's ghost exited Welsh's body. Welsh fell to his knees gasping for air, trying to get his composure back while the Warden and Albright looked on in a state of shock.

"See Albright we have a ghost," the Warden explained. The frozen windows melted and his office door swung open with Ms. Castile standing there in the doorway.

"I will go talk to the Governor, but I know he want believe this," Albright explained, walking pass Ms. Castile.

Chapter 22

Albright's own words actually sealed his fate by an incarcerated spirit because Daniel did not want anyone to know about his actions. Mr. Albright exited the Warden's outer office, leaving the Warden and Welsh together dangling their thoughts.

As Albright walked down the back stairs to the underground tunnel leading to the prison parking lot; Myers, a guard from the old Northville Prison stood guard at his post. The fairly lit walkway stretched twenty-five yards from the stairway door to the gate which led to the outside parking lot. Myers leaned back in his chair reading the newspaper. Albright was talking to himself, trying to figure out how he would explain these things to the Governor. Now, halfway to Myers he decided to stop and call the Governor on his cell phone. But there was no reception, only static. Hanging his phone up he continued to walk towards Myers. Strangely enough, he could not hear his own footsteps as he looked down and by that time Myers had lifted his eyes from the newspaper spotting Albright.

Finally, Albright reached Myers.

"Man, I didn't here you coming, you must walk really light in those wood sole shoes," Myers cracked.

Suddenly, they saw a slowly moving mist like fog approaching them from the other end of the tunnel. Both watching as it inched closer. Albright touched the door and it burnt his hand.

"Ah shit, it burns," Albright yelled. Finally, the fog reached them and the image of a lion gave an enormous roar, feeling the wind from its mouth then dissipated.

"What was that?" Myers asked.

"I do not know, but were you here four years ago," Albright asked.

"Yes, why do you ask," Myers replied.

"Never mind," Albright responded.

The door knob leading to the parking lot was to hot to touch. So they decide to go back through the tunnel.

Chapter 23

Heading down the tunnel a waterfall of blood formed in their path with dead souls floating in it. Quickly, they turned to get away from it.

However, another waterfall of blood appeared in front of them trapping them in the middle of hell.

Looking around in despair, as both of the waterfalls started moving in closer to them Myers had a bright idea that constituted jumping through the waterfall to safety, but Albright was skeptical. Myers extended his arm through the water to test it first, but when he withdrew his arm it was gone without any physical pain.

He went into shock, making him slip head first into the waterfall he touched. Quickly, he jolted back out with no head moving around like a chicken, then, fell back in. Unable to move, Albright watched the waterfall consume Myers. It's over Albright thought, putting his hands over his face to brace for his death.

But, the water's disappeared leaving no sign of Myers' body. He moved his hands, took a deep breathe, jolted to the door, and kicked it open. His eyes had to adjust because of the bright sun catching a glimpse of his car parked in the parking lot. He ran for it.

The road that divided the prison from the parking lot used by employees only Albright had to run across. Suddenly, an eighteen wheeler came roaring down this employee used road.

Quickly, the trucks' horn blew making Albright turned to see what was coming. His face paled with fear. However, it was too late for redemption. The truck hit Mr. Albright with incredible force spreading his dust remains into the air then disappeared.

Looking out of his window, the Warden observed everything, Albright running across the road, the truck striking him, turning into dust, and the truck vanishing. The Warden closed the blinds and mumbled; "We are never leaving this prison alive," sitting down into his chair and fell a sleep.

Chapter 24

As 5:00 o'clock rolled around Ms. Castile was leaving for the day. She peeped in too say good-bye and noticed that the Warden was still sleeping. Easing the door shut she proceeded through the outer office into the hallway.

Down the hallway Ms. Castile suddenly remembered that she didn't pick up the Warden's mail from the mail room two floors down. So she detoured. At the mailroom's entrance she reached over a four foot door to unlock the latch to enter.

Surprising her was Monk, behind a stack of mail bags working late shift in the mail room as a sorter.

"Well, how are you, Ms. Castile?" Monk asked, seductively, staring her up and down.

"I forgot the Warden's mail," Ms. Castile replied.

"Oh, the Warden wouldn't like that. He may punish you, over and over and over," Monk stated, as he walked closer to her. He placed his arm around her to lock the small door, as she moved away.

Suddenly, Monk reached for her blouse, ripping it off forcing her to the floor.

The time for penetration was at hand. However, mailbags started falling on top of him, breaking his concentration. Ms. Castile eased away into a corner as the onslaught of mail bags continued to strike Monk.

Suddenly, the attack stopped and Monk was caught with his pants down. He waited for another attack but there was none, so he looked over at Ms. Castile, anxious to return to what he attempted before being interrupted. His left foot struck the floor first and then his right as he drew closer to Ms. Castile with lust.

Suddenly, envelopes began to fly around the small room almost hitting Monk. The envelopes began changing from paper envelopes into spiraling blades right before their eyes. The blades were like a squad of jet planes hovering in the air over monk staring at him.

"Swoosh," they attached.

Through the air the blades with force struck the legs of Monk, dropping him to his knees.

Seven blades struck Monk after that. Two of them went in his chest right under his heart, two went through his arms like butter leaving him maimed, and three stuck in his head. Monk fell dead in between the legs of Ms. Castile. Petrified, she pushed Monk away from her enabling her to get up. While the blades hovered above Monk's body. She ran to the small mailroom door that separated her from the living and the dead to unlock it and escape.

Suddenly, Daniel's ghost appeared and she stopped with fright.

"You can go," Daniel spoke, with thoughts of his own mother running through his mind. Ms. Castile left the mail room looking back and returning to Northville Prison again. Daniel disappeared as Monk's body lay on the icy cold floor of the mail room with envelopes stuck in him and his body parts next to him.

Suddenly, the hovering envelopes turned into confetti and the other envelopes that were in Monk's body unfolded, stretching themselves around his body and his body parts. After a few seconds, Monk's body was completely wrapped by the envelopes.

They started squeezing tighter and tighter until the mid size man was no more than a tooth pick. After a few seconds he vanished from the mail room.

Chapter 25

Friday morning and the Warden had basically spent the entire week at the prison, never going home. Derrick out of the hole sat quietly in his cell. Newly hired guards canvassed the tier as the inmates laid back, not really doing anything as Matthew walked pass Derrick's cell, then retraced his steps stopping at Derrick's cell bars.

Matthew tried to cut Derrick like a knife with his eyes waiting on him to raise his head. Suddenly, Derrick raised his eyes and stared back at Matthew. Matthew said, "I'm not scared of you or your ghost. I'm going to kill you bitch." Derrick rose without being possessed by Daniel, with courage in his veins and walked over to Matthew.

"I told you I don't know what you are talking about," Derrick stated, standing toe to toe with Matthew. Matthew wanted to reply with aggression, as he made a fist to strike Derrick.

Suddenly, one of the new guards walked pass and asked, "Is everything good here?"

"Yeah, everything is straight," Matthew stated, staring at Derrick as he walked away. Derrick faded back into his cell, and began staring at the floor. The guard stood watching Derrick, as he stared at the floor.

"Derrick Samuel, I know that name sounded familiar. We went to high school together," the new guard stated, as he made one step towards Derrick.

"Anthony Wellington," Derrick replied, as he raised his head from the floor.

"Yeah, yeah, it's me in the flesh," Wellington answered.

"Well, Anthony as a long lost friend, I advise you to leave this place," Derrick spoke, with very much concern.

"Leave, I just started here and I like my job," Wellington replied.

Wellington walked away and Derrick repeated, "Leave this place." Wellington turned to reply, but a strong cold wind challenged his hair, sending a frightful chill through his entire body. Wellington looked around for a few seconds fixing his hair in the process. Derrick's eyes still planted down at the floor as he walked away.

Chapter 26

Now, in Warden Verdana's office the phone rung waking him. Verdana reached for the receiver not knowing it was the Governor concerned about Mr. Albright not reporting back the day before. "Warden this is Governor Wyatt. Have you seen Mr. Albright?"

"The last time I saw him sir, was yesterday when he left my office," Verdana replied.

"One of my staff drove by the prison last night and Mr. Albright's car was still in the parking lot," the Governor stated.

"Well, maybe it didn't start or something. All I know is that he left my office yesterday," Verdana spoke.

"Warden, were you aware that we were considering replacing you once Mr. Albright returned with his evaluation?" Governor Wyatt asked.

"No sir, I wasn't aware of that change," the Warden replied.

"Since; I haven't been able to reach Mr. Albright. I will come to the prison around 7:00 am on Sunday," the Governor stated.

"Why on Sunday sir?" Verdana asked.

"This will avoid attention to the prison until we get to the bottom of things," the Governor explained.

"We will be expecting you sir," Verdana replied.

The Warden placed the phone on the base and in anger threw everything that wasn't tided down off of his desk on to the floor. His favorite clock hit the floor hard bouncing and hit the wall, showing 9:30 am as he stared at it.

"Ms. Castile!" the Warden screamed.

After a few seconds had elapsed and there was still no reply from Ms. Castile. The Warden walked to the door trying not to step on his things that covered the floor, and opened it. Looking around for Ms. Castile he could actually hear a faint echo of his own breathing. Canvassing the room further, he noticed her computer off, her chair hadn't been pulled out from under her desk, and her desk calendar hadn't been flipped to Friday. This occurrence did not settle well with the Warden, due to the fact that Ms. Castile always called in if she couldn't make it. The Warden walked back into his office plopped himself down in his chair and rocked back and forth, staring out into the outer office where Ms. Castile should have been.

Chapter 27

Night had fallen on the tier and everyone rested their way to sleep. Except for Matthew, his heart filled with rage directed at Derrick. He couldn't wait for the guards to make their rounds. Through the prison's black market, Matthew had purchased some kerosene from one of the crooked guards. He waited patiently for the same guard who acquired the kerosene for him to come by and override the cell bars to let him out. Derrick sat on the edge of his bunk doing something with his hands while his lips moved.

Strangely, enough it mimicked the same thing that Matthew did in his cell. Rotating the kerosene cocktail in his hand and mumbling words of death about Derrick.

Hearing the guard footsteps, Matthew's happiness went to another level. The guard reached for his keys and Derrick rose from his bed and walked to the back wall of his cell and waited. The nervous guard frightened of Matthew dropped his keys on the tier floor, while trying to place them back on his belt. Disturbed some of the inmates, but did not wake them.

"Never again Matthew, this is the last time I do anything for you," the guard stated.

"You are going to do what ever I tell you, bitch as guard. Now take this money, with your crooked ass," Matthew replied.

"Do you want me to lock the cell back?" the guard asked.

"If you lock it back, how in the hell will I be able to get back in once this is done," Matthew asked.

"Yeah you right," the guard stated.

"Take you dumb ass back down to the guard's desk, before I burn your ass up," Matthew ordered, with a look of joy on his face.

With the kerosene cocktail in his hand, Matthew walked slowly to Derrick's cell. When he reached the cell bars Derrick literally rested on the back wall with his back against it. His feet placed flat on the wall with toes pointing down towards the floor possessed.

"Look what I got for you evil motherfucker," Matthew spoke.

Derrick raised his head from his quiet prayer with his eyes glowing green.

Suddenly, Matthew lit the wick and threw the bottle into the cell, breaking it. Fire subdued the entire cell and Derrick, while Matthew cheered saying, "Burn bitch burn." The other inmates woke from the smell of smoke and began yelling, "Fire." Matthew watched as Derrick walked towards him.

Surprisingly, out of the flames Derrick's hands grabbed the cell bars and stared at Matthew; the fire raging behind him and on him. Matthew, stood petrified but he mustard all his strength to say again, "Burn bitch burn."

An unearthly smile embedded Derrick's face as the guards responded. Derrick's head turned towards the end of the tier walk way as he heard them coming. Then, he turned his head back to stare in the eyes of Matthew and then faded back into the fire. Matthew watched the fire disappeared right in front of his eyes, leaving only a little smoke. Surprisingly, the things inside the cell, or Derrick were not burned. Witnessing this, Matthew ran back to his cell before the guards could see him out of his cell closing his cell bars. Derrick covered his face with both hands knowing that he was possessed.

Chapter 28

The guards arrived at Derrick's cell and noticed nothing out of the ordinary. Although, one of the guards touched the cell bars and burnt his hands.

Derrick did not move. The guards opened the cell and walked in shining their lights all around trying to find out why the cell bars where so hot. Only in Derrick's cell for only a few seconds, their boots began to melt from the hot floor.

"My boots are melting!" one of the guards yelled.

"What the fuck is happening here?" Wellington asked. Derrick finally moved when he heard Wellington's voice, turning his head towards him.

"Leave this place," Derrick spoke, still possessed. The guards asked him what had happened and Derrick replied, "I don't know, I was asleep." "Well there's nothing to do in here. Everything seems to be in order except for the hot bars and floor," Wellington spoke. So the guards turned and left the cell with Wellington trailing.

Suddenly, Derrick rose from his bed possessed and grabbed Wellington's hand and flashes of the brutal murder of Daniel Gordon filled Wellington's mind. After a few seconds Wellington pulled away from Derrick, perspiring and stunned.

"Leave this place," Derrick spoke, again able to over power the evil for a moment then Daniel left him. Wellington grabbed his baton and closed the cell bars behind him.

During Wellington's walk down the tier, a migraine headache stopped him in his tracks, making him grab for the railing. Again the thoughts of the murder, flashed through his mind. Derrick's ghost did not want to kill Wellington, like he did the other guards. Wellington was Derrick's friend. Daniel just wanted him to know what had happened to him. However, Daniel did not know the weakness of Wellington's mind. Wellington could not control the screams of murder. They overwhelmed him. When he arrived at the steps to walk down the visions became too much for him, making him grab his head, losing his balance, and falling twenty steps down to the bottom of the tier, breaking his neck.

Derrick rose, clinging to his cell bars as he heard the screams of his old high school friend as he fell.

Derrick walked over to his sink, stopping it up, and water splashed on his face.

Suddenly, Daniel's ghost face appeared in the water.

"Derrick was weak; I didn't want him to die. He didn't do anything to me," Daniel's ghost stated; as the waves in sink moved his face around???then he disappeared.

Down at the bottom of the tier Derrick could hear all the guards forming and the Warden's voice elevating over them all.

"Where is Derrick Samuel?" the Warden yelled. Derrick walked to his cell bars.

"He's in his cell sir," Chief Welsh stated.

Suddenly, the Warden spoke, "Daniel Gordon was innocent," turning around in a three hundred and sixty degree circle as if he was possessed.

"Daniel Gordon, sir, we don't have a Daniel Gordon here," one of the guards stated. The Warden walked away as Chief Welsh mumbled, "Yes we do."

Chapter 29

Chief Welsh ordered the men to take Wellington to the morgue, while the Warden walked slowly towards the bars leading off the tier.

Suddenly, the floor shook as if an earth quake occurred and then a loud shrieking noise filled the tier. One of the guards yelled, "Earthquake," his voice vibrating.

Chief Welsh turned to him and said, "That's not an earthquake son, that's evil." Then, the earthquake halted. Overhearing Chief Welsh's statement the Warden dropped his head and walked away. The guard stood dazed and confused about what Chief Welsh had stated.

"Move!" Chief Welsh yelled, as the guards moved Wellington to the morgue. For a moment, Chief Welsh looked up at the top of the tier at Derrick's cell and then left the tier.

Derrick sat on the edge of his bunk and Daniel's ghost possessed him again making him rise and walk over to the cell bars.

Impulsively, Derrick spoke, "Matthew, Matthew." Matthew rose from his bunk and stepped to his cell bars. No one heard Derrick, but they could hear Matthew.

"What do you what motherfucker?" Matthew asked.

"My turn next."

"Leave me alone, you evil bastard," Matthew screamed, shaking his cell bars.

"My turn next, my turn next, my turn next," Derrick spoke, over and over until Matthew fell to his floor screaming with his arms crossed, rocking insanely. The guards scrambled to Matthew's cell finding him emotionally distraught. They placed him in a straight jacket, and took him to the infirmary. Derrick walked back to his bunk lying down with his hands behind his head, smirking.

Chapter 30

Now, back at the Governor's mansion, the Governor was receiving a phone call about a quarter to eleven that woke him up. Gazing over at his wife, he turned over, grabbed his glasses off of the night stand, and picked up the phone.

"This better be good." the Governor spoke, as he adjusted the phone to his ear.

"Governor," Albright spoke, on the other end of the phone.

"Albright is that you?" the Governor asked, placing his feet flat on his floor?

"Yes sir," Albright replied.

"Where have you been son? We found your car in the prison's parking lot," the Governor stated.

The phone began to get really cold in his hand making the Governor have to change hands looking at the phone then placing back to his ear.

"Is there a problem sir?" Albright asked.

"No, no, continue," the Governor replied.

"Well, sir everything is under control out at the prison and Warden Verdana should be able to stay," Albright stated.

"That's good son, I'm going out there on Sunday," the Governor replied.

"No need sir," Albright stated.

"Where are you son," the Governor asked.

"I'm in my house in my bed," Albright replied.

Suddenly, the phone became frigid again, this time making the Governor drop it to the floor and grasp his hand. When it hit the floor it unleashed a loud static making the Governor place his hands over his ears and the neighborhood dogs bark uncontrollably.

The sound echoed through his bedroom for a few seconds not disturbing his wife and then subsided. He picked up the phone to call back and there were only four letters spelling one word that showed up on the phones caller ID.

"Hell."

Governor Wyatt blinked his eyes to focus and then Albright's number appeared and he listened as the phone rung.

"Hello," Mrs. Albright spoke, in a sleepy voice.

"Mrs. Albright, can I speak to your husband. We were disconnected," the Governor asked

"That's impossible sir, he hasn't been home since he left this morning. I figured he was working late at the office," Mrs. Albright stated.

The Governor became speechless; as he held the receiver against his cheek believing what he was hearing.

"Governor, Governor," Mrs. Albright bellowed.

"Thanks Mrs. Albright he probably called from the office. I just dialed the wrong number. You get some rest," the Governor stated.

They hung up their phones at the same time and Daniel's evil essence catapulted through the phone line all the way back to the prison.

Chapter 31

Saturday morning, bright and early the unrestrained Matthew rose from his infirmary bed headed for the wash room at the rear of the infirmary that had a window looking out on the yard.

Inside the washroom were three sinks, three toilets, one shower, and a twenty foot mirror that stretched horizontally above the three sinks. Matthew had his freedom of being alone.

With his toothbrush in one hand Matthew reached the washroom and hatred still in his heart for Derrick. After placing his tooth brush on the sink his next stop was the stall fragmented with sexual words written on the door.

Sitting there Matthew began hearing tiny sounds of glass breaking.

"Who's there?" Matthew yelled, nervously, then the noise stopped.

Like a cat ready to scatter when it sees a dog.

Matthew pulled up his pants without shaking hands with the toilet paper. He eased the door open and peered out and everything seemed quite. Matthew walked to the sink and started brushing his teeth. Out of the blue, a guard walked in to check up on him.

"Hurry up Matthew. I want you back in the bed." the guard ordered.

"Sure slick," Matthew replied, turning back to the mirror.

Finishing his ritual with his teeth, Matthew dropped his clothes and jumped into the shower. Several minutes passed as the steam from the shower laid wait on the twenty foot mirror stretched across the sink.

He turned the knob off and stepped out on to the semi-slippery tile floor drying off slowly walking towards the sink. He knotted the towel around his waist and reached up to clear the steam from off the mirror with his hand.

Suddenly, while reaching down to tighten his towel the face of Daniel Gordon appeared in the mirror. But when Matthew lifted his head the image disappeared.

Looking into the mirror applying shaving cream Matthew noticed a small crack forming from one end of the mirror to the other end passing right in front of his face. Matthew stepped back and the entire mirror cracked sending a loud noise through the washroom, then exploded crashing to the floor into thousands of pieces. Petrified, Matthew stood in the middle of the washroom with nothing but pieces of mirror surrounding him.

"What to do," he thought, canvassing the room.

After pondering, Matthew started walking cautiously trying not to cut himself on the pieces out of the washroom. Looking down he began witnessing imagines of Daniel's ghost in all the pieces of mirror on the floor.

Suddenly, a voice spoke, "My turn now." Matthew turned in a three hundred degree circle trying to pin point the source of the words. Completing his surveillance Matthew took out for the exit. Reaching the exit, pieces of the mirror from the floor met him blocking the doorway forming a barrier. His body's reflection distorted as if he was looking into a mirror at the circus. Matthew tried to destroy the mirror a few times with his bare feet, but it did not break, it only left his feet bleeding. Turning around, he faced the other pieces of mirror on the floor catching a glimpse of a towel bar hanging in the shower. Walking over to the towel rack,

Matthew with all of his strength pulled the towel bar from the wall. His heart beat settled down a little bit because he had found him a weapon.

"Come on, you evil motherfucker," Matthew yelled, as he stood in a defensive stand.

Again, the words emanated more forcefully.

"My turn now."

Unexpectedly, the mirror pieces on the floor started pulsated. The pieces moved across the floor forming three piles in the middle. Matthew stepped slowly towards the three piles of dormant mirror. He poked the piles, but they did not move. With a second chance to escape, he walked over to the mirror made door striking it.

Suddenly, he heard the breaking noise again in between his pounding and slowly turned to face it. When Matthew turned around he saw something that made chills run down his entire body. The three piles of mirror had formed into three mean and viscous pit bulls. The dogs walked towards him foaming at the mouth. One of the dogs leaped at Matthew; with his quick reflexes he used the towel bar to break it into pieces.

"All right, I use to beat dogs for a living," Matthew yelled, thinking he was down to two dogs. The second dog leaped at Matthew with its sharp claws striking Matthew in his chest. He grabbed his chest and fell to one knee.

In great pain Matthew looked pass the first fallen dog and the pile of mirror formed into two more dogs totaling four.

Now, another dog lunged at Matthew knocking him to the floor on to his back trying to attack his throat but he jammed the bar into his mouth wrestling on the floor until its whip like tail struck him on the side of his head cutting his ear off. Some how Matthew knocked the dog off of him and limped to the wall of mirror still blocking his exit severely injured.

The four dogs growled as they moved closer to him resting his back on the door made of mirror. Suddenly, hands stretched from out of the mirror grabbing his arms and legs subduing him as blood dripped from his ear and chest stopping the dogs' assault on him.

Suddenly, the dogs took a few steps back, formed a row, closed their eyes, and waited. Matthew dropped the towel bar awakening the dogs from their slumber. They leaped at Matthew with the image of Daniel Gordon in their mirror reflection. Two of the dogs ripped Matthew arms off and the other two ripped his legs off. Matthew did not die instantly; something was keeping him alive as the hands held the rest of his body.

While the dogs ate Matthew's extremities, Daniel's ghost spoke, "My turn next Matthew." As Matthew moved his eyes around the washroom half dead.

Soon, the hands released Matthew and the four dogs surrounding him leaving his arms and legs unattended.

With no arms or legs Matthew could only turn his head?as they stood over him slobbering ready to finish him off.

"No!" Matthew yelled, as the four dogs lounged ripping him apart.

"Matthew, you better be walking out," the guard yelled, walking towards the washroom. As he neared the mirror door and mirror dogs disappeared back into the twenty foot mirror over the sink. The guard walked in the washroom and couldn't believe his eyes. Matthew's body parts where evenly distributed into each of the three sinks, with no sign of any blood.

"Code red," the guard yelled. All guards responded to the call. One by one, they arrived heaving up their breakfast, as they gazed upon a pure act of evil. Warden Verdana was the last one to arrive, moving Chief Welsh to the side so he could see.

"We are damned," the Warden spoke.

"We are not damned Warden, we are in hell," Welsh replied.

"Well, get it cleaned up Chief and meet me in my office in an hour."

Moving Matthew's body parts from the washroom the guards did not notice a piece of the mirror under a stall. However, when they exited the washroom the missing piece of mirror floated through the air placing itself in its rightful place. Chief Welsh caught a quick glimpse of the evil because he headed up the rear. He walked over to the mirror, ran his hand across it and it seemed smooth.

"I must be seeing things," Welsh stated, under his breathe activating the faucets. The sinks were overflowing as he tried to turn them off. First, he tried the hot water, but it wouldn't turn off.

Then, Welsh tried the cold water knob and ice formed on his hand moving up his arm while the face of Daniel Gordon appeared in the mirror.

Suddenly, the ice overwhelmed his entire body but a guard came back for him.

"Chief, are you all right," the guard spoke, snapping Welsh out of this illusion.

"Yeah, yeah I'm all right. Let's go," Welsh replied, walking quickly out of the washroom shoving the guard out of the way. Unafraid of being noticed Daniel Gordon's ghost floated around inside of the mirror for awhile, and then vanished.

Chapter 32

Chief Welsh walked into Warden Verdana's outer office and noticed that Ms. Castile was not at her desk. He entered the Warden's office and asked, "Warden, where is Ms. Castile?"

"I haven't seen her since Thursday. However she left a message on the office voice mail that she had quit. She said she saw Monk die in the mail room as well as Daniel Gordon's ghost. She also said that this place was condemned," the Warden stated.

"You believe her sir," Welsh asked.

"Well, I wouldn't have a while ago, but now I truly do," the Warden replied, sitting down looking out of the window.

"So what did you want sir," Welsh asked, taking a seat.

"It looks like we are the last two alive," strolling through the computer file on Daniel Gordon.

"Derrick Samuel is the key. If we get rid of him I believe we are home free," Welsh stated.

"Chief Welsh, did we ever find the documents that inmate Chris told us Daniel held," the Warden asked.

"No sir," Welsh replied.

"Well, I believe Derrick Samuel knows where they are. So find them and then we'll figure out a way to get rid of Derrick Samuel," the Warden stated.

"Yes sir," Welsh replied, rising from his seat and walking out of the door.

Back on the tier things were very quite. Most of the inmates did not want to leave the sanctuary of their jail cells. The recreation area was empty except for one guard playing solitaire in front of the television monitor.

In his cell Derrick rested on his bunk reading one of the books left behind by Daniel years ago.

Suddenly, the ghost appeared on the page and spoke, "In the wall behind the mirror, you will find a zip lock bag and in the bag there's a disk."

Derrick closed the book and rose to find the disk. Daniel's ghost hovered next to him as he walked over to the mirror. It was a difficult task to loosen the mirror from the wall. It had been years since the mirror had been hanging there without being moved. Derrick nudged, pulled, and finally the mirror was free from the wall. He stuck his hands through the dark hole meeting with a few unwanted bugs.

Quickly, Derrick pulled his hands out with the disk in a zip lock bag clinging to his fingers. He wiped the bag clean from the four years of dust and mildew. Daniel's ghost spoke, "This is what I died for," then faded away.

Chapter 33

Chief Welsh was trying to figure out how to kill Derrick back in his office. But not before he found the information that Daniel had hide.

Around 8:00 o'clock pm Welsh loaded a thirty-eight caliber hand gun to carry on to the tier as the sun made its way to wake up the moon. There were inmates who were finishing their evening duties. Chief Welsh slammed his desk drawer, placed his thirty-eight in his ankle hoister and proceeded to the tier waiting for lights out. Welsh wanted everyone down for the night before he took Derrick out of his cell to question him about Daniel's information. He wanted to keep his sins away from the prying eyes of the inmates.

He proceeded down a long corridor, as if anger and fear had taken control of him.

Suddenly, from the shadows six dead inmates surrounded him...their eyes glowing green.

"What the hell are you?" the Chief yelled.

Suddenly, inside the circle the ghost of Daniel floated around him. Chief Welsh reached down grabbing his thirty-eight from his ankle and fired until his gun hammer slammed back. The bullets did not touch Daniel; they just hovered in the air and melted to the floor. Then, the ghost vanished. The words, "Shots fired," emanated from Chief Welsh's radio. Quickly, he responded to the call while the six inmates surrounded him.

"Help me. It's me. It's a riot, lock down the prison," Welsh yelled.

"Are you all right Chief," the guard asked, on the other end of the radio.

"East corridor, under attack," the Chief yelled.

Loud noises of cell bars being locked resounded through the entire prison. Moving in on Welsh the six undead inmates began beating him. Breathing his last breathe the guards arrived, however, the undead were gone leaving Chief Welsh on the floor beaten to death.

While the guards stood over Welsh the lights in the entire prison went out and a grayish cloud outside descended down on the prison.

Suddenly, the cell bars opened releasing all the inmates. There weren't enough guards to stop them from destroying everything in their path while trying to escape. Derrick did not try to escape he rested on his bunk as inmates ran pass his cell. In his office, Warden Verdana heard the havoc on his radio.

Then, the rioting inmates, the guards, the rats, and bugs fell fast to sleep leaving only Warden Verdana and Derrick Samuel awake.

The Warden's radio went silent. Hysterical, he checked different channels to reach Chief Welsh, but only static raged.

Chapter 34

Meanwhile, on the tier sleeping bodies were all over the place as Derrick sat still on his bed. Unsuspectingly, Daniel's ghost materialized and possessed Derrick again. Derrick rose with the disk in his hand and walked out of his cell.

The Warden after not being able to reach anyone over the radio he left his office on his way to the tier. The Warden turned the corner stepping over unconscious bodies and spotted Welsh's body laying on the floor in the corridor beaten to death. When he looked up, Derrick stood at the other end of the corridor. Warden Verdana froze in place as the eyes of Derrick glowing greener.

"You shall reap what you sew," thundered the voice of Daniel through the mouth of Derrick. Slowly, the possessed Derrick began to walk towards Verdana and with every foot step he landed on a body, breaking arms and legs. Warden Verdana turned and ran, but doors and bars closed on him.

Finally, he reached the door to the yard and it opened. Derrick made his way from out of the corridor around to the next.

Suddenly, before Verdana could reach the door. The arm of Derrick stretched about forty feet down the corridor almost grabbing him. But he closed the door behind him and Derrick's hand rammed into the steel door with so much force placing a fist imprint in the door. Warden Verdana ran down the ramp into the middle of the yard, looking around trying to find a place to run.

The steel door flew open, the ground rumbled, and Derrick walked out of it. Warden Verdana tried to run, however, out of the ground grew stone pillars ten feet tall surrounding the entire yard. The entrance gates melted together, the barbed wire circling the prison grew larger and heavier making it crash to the ground. Verdana was trapped with Derrick on his tail.

He turned around and Derrick with his green eyes stood in his face. Verdana could not move, because Derrick controlled his body.

Derrick's eyes became greener to enhance the images of Daniel's death like a television. He hypnotized Verdana to make him see and feel Daniel's pain four years ago.

Derrick's eyes closed and opened abruptly. But this time they were clear. Derrick rubbed his face to wake up from his possessed sleep.

"Warden," Derrick spoke.

"I can not move, help me," the Warden asked.

Suddenly, Daniel's ghost emerged from out of the ground, touching the Warden and quickly moving away.

"Derrick, place my bible that's in your pocket on the ground next to the Warden," Daniel's ghost ordered. Derrick stared at the Warden, who seemed too had aged as he placed the bible down.

Then, without warning the melted gates opened and Daniel's ghost pointed to it.

"You can go Derrick," Daniel's ghost stated.

Derrick looked at the prison, then the Warden, back at Daniel's ghost, and walked backwards towards the gate, until he was out. He paused, turned around and walked away under the morning sun leaving behind the, *"Pen of Iniquity."* Daniel closed the gate and they were all alone. Verdana's had aged thirty more years as he stood motionless in the yard. Daniel's ghost placed the curse of a slow and painful death when he touched him. Daniel's ghost vanished, the stone pillars disappeared, the barbed wire reshaped to its original state, the gates and doors unlocked, and everyone in the prison awoke.

The Governor arrived at the front gate, departed his vehicle, and noticed in the distance a person that resembled Warden Verdana standing in the middle of the court yard. The guards on the guard tower were dazed and confused as they spotted the Governor.

"Who's that?" a guard asked.

The Governor looked up at the guards without saying a word.

"Oh, it's you Governor," the guard realized, as he opened the gate. The Governor started to walk towards the figure in the yard, as the guards looked on.

Finally, reaching the figure, he recognized it as being the Warden, dead of old age standing there slumped over. Walking around Verdana he found the bible on the ground with a disk in it. He bent down and pulled the disk from the bible. Suddenly, the bible opened to a page and the Governor noticed the words, "You shall reap what you sew," circled in red.

He looked up at Warden Verdana for a second and then peered down at the disk in his hand as the tower guards made their way to him. Back in the

Verdana's office, Daniel's ghost completed one more deed as he hovered over the computer. The computer flicked on and Derrick Samuel's docket file appeared, showing Derrick's face and his information. Then, the word, "Delete," appeared on the screen and Daniel's ghost pressed yes and glided around the room holding his dearly departed mother's hand and they faded away into the fore wall.

CPSIA information can be obtained at www.ICGtesting.com
Printed in the USA
LVOW06s2248030415

433254LV00001B/24/P